STARLIGHT

STARLIGHT

a collection of
short stories

HANNAH
LEE KIDDER

Edited by Krystal Dean
Cover by Damonza
Illustrations by Rosalyn Stilling (IG: @maidofthemoon)

CONTENTS

For Fuego

SLICED

A man stands under a streetlamp, watching the flickering light. His bloody mouth hangs open. His stare is still. The light clicks on and casts harsh, sharp shadows on his face. It clicks off and he's soft again, blinking. His shirt is crusted brown, layered beneath fresh red.

The man didn't always have a mouth, so he cut one himself and grew long teeth to fill it. Now he wanders the streets at night, as if he's searching for something, but he doesn't ask for help—never speaks at all. He still bleeds.

My sneaker squeaks on the pavement, echoing into the sleeping town.

His eyes snap to me. One fang glints, a tear of blood rolling down and splattering onto the sidewalk. He breathes, raspy and wet, raising a hand in greeting.

"Good evening," I say, carefully folding my hands behind my back.

His eyes smile, but his jaw hangs. He turns back to the streetlamp, and I continue on my way. A tabby picks along the sidewalk toward me. She meows, rubbing her head against my shin.

"Hi, there." I smile.

She walks a figure eight between my legs, meows again, then looks at me.

"I hope you had a lovely day," I tell her. "It's a bit cold out."

She blinks. I smile again, and she leaves.

I hold my hands in front of me and wiggle my fingers. They can move and flex, splay out and ball up. I clench them. Then spread them as far as they will go. The spaces between glisten red. I press my fingers into each other, hiding the gashes, and my hands look like everyone else's.

I glance over my shoulder at the man with the bleeding mouth. His fingers are dry, solid flesh wrapped around each.

I turn back and give a small wave to the empty street, just to try it out. A thin stream of blood trails down my arm. I keep walking and push my hands into my pockets.

INK

She runs through the night of spindly needles and crackerjack twigs. The quill in her grip bleeds black behind her.

The shadow boy is here, with a whip laugh and no name— skittering tree trunks, leaping brush like a gazelle on fire.

His infective giggle pulls her to laugh too, making her forget to be afraid.

But she remembers, and she runs.

Her ink trails, but the forest is blacker. It will not lead her home.

THE SWAMP WITCH

Marigold leans her head against the back of her rocking chair, eyes closing to swamp buzz and raven caws. She grinds herbs in a mortar and pestle by touch. Her bare feet are stretched out on the porch, warming in the setting sunlight. A June bug flies in lazy loops, knocking gently against the shack.

The slurp of boots slaps through the trees, and Marigold exhales heavily through her nose. Only one pair of feet—not a mob to torch her shack. Probably just a townee here for a favor. She doesn't open her eyes.

The steps grow louder until they stop in front of her porch.

"Madam Marie?" The woman's voice trills with a sweet southern lilt. "I'm Emily Garner. I need your help."

Marigold peeks one eye open.

A petite woman with dark hair and long lashes stands with her hands folded at her belly.

"Watchu want?" Marigold says.

"I've heard tell of your healing. I have a skin condition, see." Emily tugs up the sleeves of her yellow dress and holds out the underbelly of her arms. They're splotched red and swollen.

"Do it hurt?" Marigold asks.

"No, ma'am."

"Do it itch?"

Emily takes a shuddering inhale, like she's teetering on the edge of tears. "They're ugly, Miss Marie. Boys don't like to touch them."

"Sounds a blessing to me, Miss Garner."

Emily pulls her sleeves back to her wrists. "There's talk of your swamp mud. They say it's got healing properties."

"Girlie, if you lookin' for gangrene, go on 'n wipe some of that mud in your wounds."

Emily opens and closes her mouth. She nods softly, eyes wet. She turns, hiking her dress to her knees and stepping high to trek back through the swamp.

"Miss Garner," Marigold calls after her.

Emily peeks over her shoulder.

She dumps the ground herbs from her mortar into the tip of her pipe, a dark curl falling over her face. "It's too hot out for sleeves, honey."

Emily smiles small and keeps walking.

Marigold stamps the herb mixture down and lights it, leaning into her chair and dragging a heavy inhale. She drops her head back to release a cloud to the splintered wood planks.

The crab trap splashes back into the water like a handful of dropped pebbles.

Marigold hefts the bucket to her hip and walks with the moonlight. She picks her steps along a familiar path, toeing from low cypress knee to grass tuft to avoid sinking her feet in mud.

The crabs' pointed legs titter against the metal bucket. She sings to them. When the sun beams hottest, the swamp smells like old meat left to turn. At night, it's earthy. Marigold likes to take her walks in the dark.

A figure moves ahead of her in the trees. She silently falls in line beside them. It's a pale woman, clutching something in thick arms.

"Whoever told ya I'm a healer's been lying to you," Marigold says.

The woman yelps, tripping over her own feet but righting herself before she falls. She spins to face Marigold with a baby in her arms, its fat legs swinging at her waist.

"Are you Marie? Please, my boy's sick. I don't know where else to go."

Marigold looks at the baby's exposed legs. "I can tell ya the night swamp, uncovered like ya got him, ain't the place. Take him to a doctor."

"I don't trust all that."

"*All that* what?"

"Modern medicine…chemicals."

Marigold clunks her bucket to the ground. "But you want me to grind up some cicada shells and spit in 'em?"

The woman's eyes widen, but she doesn't look afraid. She shifts the baby to her hip. "Is that what you do?"

"I don't do healing. Take your baby to a doctor." Marigold leans forward and hisses, "Or bring him back here when he's dead. Young meat's tender."

The woman stumbles backward before scurrying into the dark.

A raven bigger than Marigold's thigh lands on the ground and caws. He reaches his neck to peck at the sliver of dead mouse.

"Hey, friend," Marigold coos from her back porch steps. She tosses another piece of meat at his feet.

He hops closer to grab it and jerks his head back, swallowing it whole.

She smiles. "That's a good boy." She holds out a live mouse, tail pinched between her fingers. The mouse wriggles, grabbing for her hand, and she shakes him back down so he can't bite her.

The raven croaks and hops closer.

"MARIE!"

The raven caws and flies away.

Marigold growls, tossing the mouse. He disappears into the grass. She shoves to her feet and stomps around the side of her shack.

A man bangs on her front door. "Marie, I have a job for you!"

"Watchu want?"

He whips to face her. His skin is sallow beneath his eyes and around his mouth. He's a big man with clenched fists. Mouse brown hair falls across his forehead, stopping short above thin eyebrows. "I need a potion for my wife."

"I ain't no healer."

"No." His voice is low, effortlessly threatening. "She's fuckin' one of my friends."

Marigold pulls her pipe from her pocket and lights it, evaluating him before hooking it between her teeth. "I might be able to do something. Gonna cost ya though."

"I've got money."

"Enough for my magic?"

He pulls a roll from his pocket and tosses it to her.

Marigold leans to snatch it from the air. "You an awful throw," she says, unwrapping the roll and counting the bills. "Need a potion for that too, white boy?"

He stares at her.

"I'ma need twice this," she says around her pipe.

He wordlessly produces another roll and hurls it straight to her.

"Have a squat on the porch. It'll be a minute." She climbs the steps, looking him up and down as she passes, and walks into her hut.

A single bulb flicks the room to life when she tugs the chain. The kitchen is small and tidy. The window above the sink helps illuminate a dark wooden table. Marigold crosses to her fireplace mantel and plucks a few of the herbs hanging above. From a shelf, she swipes three jars and tucks them under her arm. After a moment's consideration, she grabs one more.

She pulls a bowl and whisk from a drawer and slides them onto the table. The mortar and pestle are still on the porch, but she can't be bothered to fetch them. It doesn't matter—the dried herbs crush easily in her fist before she rubs her palms together, dark dust snowing into the bowl.

The jar of mushroom gel is tightly sealed, but it pops open when she taps it on the counter. She measures four careful teaspoons into the bowl, then opens the jar of spicy green beans, pulling out two with her forefinger and thumb to drop into her mouth. They're from last season—she loves them aged. She munches while she scoops measurements from the last two jars. She's considered naming her jellies and oils, but it's not like she shares recipes.

She hops onto her countertop, pulling the bowl between her legs, and whisks the mixture, picking another green bean with her free hand.

The potion is a little thick. She reaches to the sink, splashing some tap water into the bowl, and whisks again. She spits in it. Perfect.

Marigold pours the mixture into a cup and walks outside. "Here." She hands him the potion.

He stares into the cup. "Do I make her drink it?"

"No," Marigold says. "You drink it."

"What does it do?" He sniffs the cup.

She takes her time relighting her pipe, considering. "It will curse your wife with great pains if she lies with anyone but you."

"That's not enough." His shoes have left mud prints on her porch. "I want her to suffer."

"Then drink it and leave her." She takes a drag and lets it fill her lungs. "Let her live out her life alone," she puffs, "and die with no one."

He pauses a moment, then tips the cup into his mouth and swallows, Adam's apple bowing deeply. "How long does it take?"

"Oh," Marigold says, face pointing to the ceiling, smoke leaking from her nostrils.

He keels over and slaps unceremoniously into the mud.

"Not too long."

He lays on his back across her kitchen table. The bulb swings, swirling his face in its own shadows.

Marigold slips the wedding ring from his finger. He doesn't have a tan line beneath it. She unclips his watch and empties his pockets, dropping it all into a cloth sack she sets aside. His clothes don't look like they're worth much, so she strips him and tosses them into her own pile of laundry.

She jerks the ropes tucked above her cabinet. They unravel from the ceiling pulley, dropping two leather straps that she wraps around each of his ankles. She winds the rope around her wrist and yanks, hoisting him into the air.

She disengages the wheel locks on the table and pushes it aside. His body sways—probably the gentlest he's ever done anything. She slips a five-gallon bucket beneath his head and slits his throat.

She grabs her green beans and sits on the floor.

Red slides over his chin, navigating the pricks of two-day-old hairs and dripping off his cheekbones. With a little color and no sneer, she can almost imagine him handsome.

By the time she drops her empty jar into the sink, he's drained.

She seals the blood and stores it for black pudding. The electric knife reaches with an extension cord, and the plastic tarp on the floor crinkles under her feet—she didn't bother covering the table. She likes the deep hue of blood-stained wood.

Marigold doesn't often have the opportunity to use an entire body, especially one this thick, but slicing meat from bone isn't a skill your hands forget. She drops the severed flesh into a large bowl, the bones into a bucket at her feet. Her new vacuum sealer adds an extra step between butchering and freezing, but she picks it up fast, and it's quick work.

His eyeballs, organs, and tongue go into jars with preservative oils. The spleen, she sets on a plate beside her kitchen sink—she'll have that for dinner. She hefts the bone bucket onto her hip and walks outside.

Bullfrogs and cicadas sing to the setting sun. A few yards from her hut, she pulls a femur and stabs it into the mud. The ground comes alive with fire ants, swarming to cover it, like pulsing dirt.

"Eat up," she says, stabbing in another.

When she's done, the swamp is a graveyard of white, bleeding headstones.

Marigold rocks in her chair with her pipe. The raven tears into a rabbit on the porch beside her.

Sarah arrives, dressed demurely. Long, sandy hair and a high collar hide bruises Marigold knows stamp her throat. She steps onto the porch without invitation.

Marigold grabs the cloth sack of the man's belongings from the ground at her feet.

"Thank you, Marie." Sarah grips it with both hands.

Marigold puffs her pipe. "It's what I do, honey."

CONTAINED

Vent slats stare back from the ceiling, at me and my bed. Low light throws shadows into the metal box, slitting what I can see like Venetian blinds.

I wait for a face to peer out. The longer I'm awake, the clearer red eyes blink, growl rattling through the dripping razor fangs of a monster or a demon or a vampire waiting to drain my blood. My parents would find a cold corpse in the morning, my fogged eyes still watching the vent.

Sometimes it's a ragged man, living in the air system. I'm not sure how he fits, but I see his grayed beard, frayed beanie. He watches the house from every output, and when we fall asleep, he crawls out to lick crumbs from the countertops.

A clunk vibrates my room and tears my eyes away.

A hum.

The heater kicked on.

When I look back, I swear something ducks behind the duct corner, but it doesn't return.

Sometimes I worry that my stare dares them to appear. That the only thing keeping creatures locked away is my not seeing them. I should hide my eyes.

But the night ticks by, and I watch the vent.

WARM

I'd never thought of blood as warm until it was sliding down my arms and into my sleeves, dripping into my eyes from your open mouth.

I watched your life fade. Moments with family, friends you'd never see again. You were old enough to be in college and young enough that you'd never graduate.

You didn't know how your knife ended up in my hand. The surprise in your face was still there after you weren't—after you slumped, I pushed you off, and your head bounced on the concrete.

I used the belt loops you tore to pull up my pants. I left yours around your knees when I dialed for an ambulance with steady hands. Self-defense, they said a hundred times after. And it was.

But why was it so easy?

MARGROVE

"It would be a sin, Elizabeth." Lucy sat with her legs tucked beneath her and a book in her lap.

"Of course it isn't," I told her. "It's acting. You'd be just like Sarah Bernhardt." Lucy had loved Sarah Bernhardt ever since we saw her perform in Paris before Papa died. I could see her considering it, so I pressed. "This could be practice. When you're a famous stage performer, they'll all say how you started as a young woman, making up stories with your sister."

We were on our bedroom floor with Grandmother Margrove's dress spread between us. I had found it in Mother's old trunk.

"Mother would say it is sinful." She ran a finger over the delicate lacing, the scars on her hands and wrists shining white in the sun.

"Mother will never know. It can be another of our secrets, like the embroidery we sell and the hats we weave for the merchants." I reached out, squeezing her ankle. "All I need is to catch Henry's attention. Then we can be out of this house and need never worry about what Mother says again."

Lucy fretted with her gown sleeve. "I suppose we can try it," she said. "Just once."

Henry King's smoking room was dim. I sat at the head of the card table and lit three candles, only enough to light the chairs. The young men filed in.

Henry chuckled. "What are you going to do, ay, Lizzie? Distract us and pick our pockets?"

I just smiled and motioned for them to sit.

Henry sat to my left, Michael Reed to my right, and Corville DeLashe across from me. They flicked worried glances into the darkness, but Henry just looked amused.

"I sense you are a skeptic," I told him. I had a collection of newspaper clippings under my bed on Spiritualists and their performances. I was versed in the verbiage.

"You sense that, do you?" He smirked. Upon my silence, he added, "Aren't we all?"

"Try to set aside those thoughts." I pulled Grandmother's sapphire necklace from my pocket—an heirloom gift for my thirteenth birthday—and held it in the middle of our circle with a straight arm. It swung in gentle loops. "This is a talisman linked to Alice Margrove," I said. "She will speak through it." I pooled the chain on the table and left the blue stone to rest atop.

"We may all join hands." I slipped my hand into Henry's. "Spirits are attracted to those gathered in agreement." A concept I borrowed from the Holy Word, hoping God wouldn't mind, just once. "Close your eyes."

Shadows danced across the boys' faces and our clasped hands. I let them sit in the quiet for a few moments before I intoned, "Spirit world, lords and ladies of beyond, I ask you make way for my grandmother to walk among us in the realm of mortals."

Silence sat thick around us, ebbing with the swaying light.

"Someone is with us," I said. That was Lucy's cue. "Grandmother, is that you? Speak to me."

Lucy tiptoed from behind a curtain and stood by Corville. Her face was white with powder and matched the pale dress.

"I am Alice Margrove," Lucy said, voice nothing like her own. She was deep in her role. Even her face looked different, older and serious and not unlike the portraits of Grandmother Margrove.

The moment she spoke, the boys startled, whipping their heads around.

"Do not unclasp hands!" I said, making it up as I went along. "We are safe as long as we are united."

"Hello, Elizabeth," Lucy said. "I am sorry we never got to meet, but I have watched you from beyond." She paced around the table, running a dainty hand along Michael's shoulder, down to his other arm. She did the same to Corville, doubling back on her finger trail to quirk his chin. "Why have you summoned me?" The excitement of a performance seemed to have banished all thoughts of sin from Lucy's mind.

"Grandmother, what wisdom have you to impart us?" I asked.

Lucy placed a hand on Michael's forehead. "Beware the flowers," she said. "Pretty things distract from thorns." She walked to Corville and grasped him the same way. "Blue things will serve you." And Henry: "Be generous to those who offer you grace. Else you will suffer greatly."

Henry stared at Lucy, his face wet with silent tears. Skepticism gone, it seemed.

Lucy pulled her hands into herself, taking a soft step back. She watched the darkness. The boys' eyes were locked on her, so I huffed an exhale and extinguished the candles.

Michael yelped. "Grab a light!" he said. "Grab a light, grab a light!"

Someone struck a match, the acrid sulfur stinging my nose, small flame illuminating Henry's face. He lit the candles again.

Lucy was gone.

Corville slammed his fist on the table. "What trickery?"

"No tricks," I said. I held my palms open, as if that proved anything.

"Search the room, lads." He shoved his chair away and started flipping couch cushions, peering behind furniture. Michael joined him.

But they wouldn't find anything. Lucy had slipped from the room to change her clothes and join the party, as if she had been there all along.

"Was I really just like Sarah Bernhardt?" Lucy asked while we waited for the carriage. She pulled her hair ribbons in front of her face and watched me between them.

"Absolutely," I said, flicking through the tidy stack of bills Henry had slipped into my palm as we left the party. It was an unexpected but very welcome outcome. One that gave me a brand new idea. "If the boys weren't so convinced you were a spirit, they would have asked for your autograph."

She gave a small smile.

"Those weren't the lines we'd planned," I said, frowning as she shrugged guiltily. "But I believe you may have found us another way out of Mother's house." I waved the bills. "We've made quite the sum. Imagine what we can make next time." I couldn't bite back my grin.

The carriage pulled in front of us, and the driver tipped his hat. Lucy climbed in. "You mean to do this again?"

"Just a time or two more," I said. "Forget Henry. With this money and what we've already saved, we could grow my dowry. I could marry someone else, someone I actually care to wed. And you will be out in society in no time at all. Perhaps we could even save enough for you to go to London. Perform on a real stage."

The wheels crunched rocks as the carriage wobbled its way onto the road. Lucy watched the trees pass, scratching at her wrist with one fingernail.

I slipped my hand between hers. "Look at this," I said, pressing the money into her palm.

She leaned back and counted it slowly, her eyebrows rising and shoulders relaxing. "Well," she said lightly. "I suppose a time or two more couldn't hurt."

I hoisted Lucy onto the trellis and watched her scamper to our unlocked balcony door. She was small and lithe enough to pull herself up. I waited until she was safe inside to hurry to the back door.

A moment later, Lucy opened it with bare feet and a grin.

Mother had fallen asleep on her chair in the library, as she often did, with her day clothes crumpled, hair sticking every which way, and an empty bottle of something tucked in with her.

I slipped off my shoes and we crept upstairs. I changed into my nightgown.

"Where did you find Grandmother's dress?" Lucy whispered from the doorway.

"In the attic," I told her. "Why?"

She chewed her bottom lip. "Were there more of her things?"

"I believe the whole trunk was hers."

Lucy disappeared down the left hall, walking quickly— probably before she lost her nerve.

I propped myself against the doorframe with a book to wait for her return and watch down the right hall for Mother. I was sure she'd remain sleeping, but she was like a rat in the way that you'd no idea it was there until it had eaten through your cookie tin and shat on every shelf of the pantry.

Lucy appeared from the darkness again, and we locked the door behind us. Her arms were full of books.

"What are those?" I asked.

"Grandmother's journals," she said, smiling. "If we're going to do this, we're going to do it properly."

Each Sunday, Mother wore what we called her Maternal Uniform. Fully clothed, shod, hair in place under a stark white covering. She kept her rosary wrapped three times around her left wrist, cross clasped in her palm.

Lucy and I sat silently in the carriage, eyes down, hands folded, backs straight.

I could feel Mother's eyes scraping up and down us, as tangible as if she were doing it with a fork. Before breakfast, we checked each other over, head-to-toe, for a hair out of place, a button undone. It was a quick ride to the church, but she'd find something to admonish us for. She always did. Every Sunday, she'd choose one of us to torment, and it echoed through the rest of the week. Our performance would dictate our fate until the next Sunday, and the entire carriage ride was a game of waiting.

Mother sucked air between her teeth, a snake's hiss, and reached across the cab before I could stop her. She raked her nails over Lucy's hand, leaving four red streaks, two of them already bleeding.

I pulled my kerchief and pressed it to her wounds, glaring at her skirt with clenched teeth.

"If you do it yourself, what's the trouble in my helping?" Mother said lightly. We arrived at the church and she left the carriage first.

Lucy's chin trembled, but she stared ahead.

"I'm sorry, Lucy," I whispered.

"It's my own fault. She's right."

"You cannot help it," I said, pulling off my ring. I slipped it onto her finger. "When you feel the compulsion, just twist this around, okay?"

Lucy's eyes shimmered with tears, but they were dull. Slowly, she began to twist the ring.

"Chin up, little love," I said, quirking her nose.

She looked at me without an ounce of comfort before slipping from the carriage. I thought of the money stashed in my sewing kit. It wasn't enough yet.

The next Sunday, I wore ripped stockings.

Corville DeLashe invited us to a gathering of his friends from university—eight or nine men with a few ladies, most of them already drinking. I was able to set up our tricks while I mingled, with no one the wiser.

"How did you find you had this talent?" a man with a young face asked me.

I was sitting in a broad-backed chair, facing the room of guests. "It was when I found a trunk of my grandmother's belongings," I said, which was the closest to the truth I could manage. "Some clothes, old books. She just…spoke to me."

"Did she have a tragic life?"

"She did." I paused. It wasn't the sort of thing people spoke of, but if there was ever a place for it, it was there. I glanced at the door Lucy was hidden behind, unsure if she could hear me. She was too young when I'd been told the truth about Grandmother. I lowered my voice. "She was locked away," I said. "They thought her insane."

"Insane," another guest said. "Or possessed?"

I closed my eyes and shrugged a shoulder.

"Oh, a mysterious one!" someone shouted.

I wrapped Grandmother's necklace around my wrist. I stayed silent for nearly a full minute to let anxieties build, then cleared my throat. "We call upon Alice Margrove, should the spirit world allow her safe passage." I waited. "We call upon Alice Margrove!" I called louder.

Some people glanced around the room, some didn't waver their gaze from me. I slipped my foot behind the string that wrapped the leg of my chair, running beneath the rug to a candlestick across the room. I tugged, and the candlestick clattered into the one beside it.

Heads whipped around, and a woman in the back screamed.

From the dark edge of the room, I barely saw the door open and Lucy whiz past, hunched near the floor.

I stood. "I apologize, everyone." I straightened my skirts. "The spirit world is tumultuous, and these things are to be expected. It is fine, I assure you."

When the room was settled, I resumed, still on my feet and clutching the sapphire pendant in my palm.

"Grandmother," I said. "It is I, Elizabeth. You are among friends. Will you speak with us?"

A heavy moment lingered.

The young-looking man stood. "Come on, Corville," he said, a tremor of uncertainty in his voice that his dismissive chuckle couldn't quite cover. "This is silly."

Lucy's hands on my shoulders sent pinpricks down my spine. I sat, revealing her behind my chair.

The room gasped together, then fell deathly silent. The man stumbled back and tripped, falling into someone's lap.

"How may I be of service?" Lucy asked softly.

"Friends," I said, "meet Alice."

Lucy gave a showstopping performance. She stayed behind my chair the whole time, hands on my shoulders as if I were anchoring her there.

The audience questioned her—about her previous life, spirits, how she could cross between existences. Lucy improvised the most convincing speeches, weaving in facts about Grandmother—even I was enthralled with the world she built. It was truly enchanting.

A lady with a modest gown and dark hair approached my chair, kneeling before it. She folded both of her hands in front of her. "Mrs. Margrove, my name is Harriet. Do you interact with other souls, on that side?"

"I meet many," Lucy said.

"Was there ever a woman named Eloise Tailor amongst them?"

I watched the lace running I'd pulled close to the fire earlier. It was just beginning to smoke.

"Ah," Lucy said. "Eloise. She remains strong, and she encourages you to do the same."

Harriet pressed her hands to her heart and nodded graciously. "Thank you, Mrs. Margrove."

Lucy stepped around my chair, running her hand down my arm and lacing fingers with mine. She smiled at Harriet. "Call me Alice."

The runner sprang to lively fire, flames licking along the mantel in seconds.

I sprang to my feet as someone shouted, "Fire!"

Many people ran from the room. A woman fainted. Corville dumped a vase of flowers on the flames, dragging the fabric to the ground and stomping it dead.

When the commotion settled, no one had seen Lucy slip from the window.

Our ruse went on for months. We played smaller and smaller crowds, performing personal conjurings for the rich and mourning. This made the theatrics of it a bit trickier but worked in our favor to keep Mother unaware.

But there was the trouble of Lucy coming to the age that she should be properly out in society. To keep people from seeing Lucy and connecting her to Alice, we made that Lucy was sickly.

"We've had doctor after doctor examine her," Mother said woefully. She petted Lucy's hair, pushing her head into the pillow.

Lucy looked at me where I sat at my desk, and I crossed my eyes at her. The corner of her mouth twitched.

"You poor darling," Mrs. Vance said. She held one hand to her heart, while the other pressed a kerchief to her nose. "You are on our prayer list."

Mother bowed her head graciously, then motioned to the door. "Do you have time for tea?"

They left as abruptly as they'd entered.

Lucy pushed the blankets off and sat up. "I have never received this much attention in my life."

"How is it?" I smiled and turned back to my book.

"Splendid," she said, pulling out the satchel of herbs Mrs. Vance had shoved under her neck. She sniffed it and wrinkled her nose before tossing it away.

I thought Lucy might grow tired of staying hidden, but her time in the light as Alice was more than enough to keep her satiated. No, not satiated—she was thrilled. And Mother adored having an ill daughter to talk about at tea.

The money was substantial, and we had more than enough for my dowry. I found a performance school in London for Lucy. We had nearly enough for her to go. A few months more, and we could be free.

On some occasions, I was invited out as a guest, not a performer. Lucy remained home and covered for me if Mother sought me out. I hated to leave her, but the charade had become a full-time occupation. A necessary evil to add to my list of them.

I was on the balcony one such night, my shoes tucked under my arm. Only Lucy could climb up, but I had no issue descending.

"When will you be back?" Lucy was in the doorway.

"I won't be long," I told her. "It's just one of those parties where men like to impress their guests with other guests. I will gather a few clients and leave."

Lucy nodded quietly. She twisted the ring on her finger.

I pulled back from the railing and brushed a hand on her cheek. "We will play cards when I return, okay?"

She nodded and pressed her hand to her throat, looping a finger around the chain there, toying with a blue stone pendant.

"Is that—" I swept her hand away. "Lucy!" I whipped her around by her shoulders and unclasped the chain. I watched Grandmother's necklace in my hand. "You've been through my things?"

"You never wear it," she said. "You only use it as a prop." She twisted the ring on her finger again, faster.

"How could you take it?" I gripped it tight in my palm. We borrowed each other's things all the time, but the necklace was special. I stomped back inside to lay it in my memory box and slam the lid.

"It's beautiful," she said, "and it's mine anyway."

I frowned. "It is mine. Mother gave it to me, before…" I pushed past her and climbed from the balcony. "It's mine, Lucy. Don't touch it again."

"The painters found scuffs on the trellis," Mother said.

I took an extra large bite of dinner to have the excuse of chewing while I thought up a response, but Mother was looking at Lucy.

"What have you been doing?" Mother asked. "Running the streets at night like a stray cat?"

Lucy said nothing.

I swallowed and said, "Oh, Mother. She isn't a child anymore. I haven't even seen her climb a tree in ages." I tried to make my laugh easy.

Mother's eyebrows lifted so high they neared her hairline. She watched Lucy for an answer.

"Running the streets." Lucy smirked. "What a thought. Though, you might consider it." She stood from the table and quirked a finger under Mother's chin. "Maybe a cookie or two fewer with tea, as well."

The red rose in Mother's cheeks, and I prayed for a tantrum. But she made no sound, which was far worse.

Lucy, what have you done?

"Is the trellis damaged, Mother?" I kept my voice steady. "Or can they simply paint over it? Now that you mention it, I have been seeing a few neighborhood children playing around our yard, perhaps they—"

Before I could stand, Mother had both hands wrapped around Lucy's hair like a mariner tightening ropes to hoist a sail, and Lucy screamed.

I hurried after them as Mother dragged her down the hallway, Lucy's legs flailing and slipping on the slick wood floors.

"Mother, please—" I looped my arms around Lucy's abdomen to carry her weight by something other than her hair. "Lucy is unwell! Perhaps she has another fever. Let me bring her to bed—"

Mother stepped into me and growled in my face. "Release her or join her."

My fingers slackened, and I watched her drag Lucy away. Her screams disappeared up the stairs.

It was better to have one of us loose.

Mother drank herself to sleep that night, giving me free run of the kitchen to gather anything I could cut thinly enough to fit under the bolted attic door.

I sat on the floor, slipping slices of cured ham and ribbons of carrot to Lucy's needy fingers. Beside me was the lantern I'd brought to shine between the cracks, because I knew well that the darkness was the worst of it all.

I dropped my forehead to the door. "Are you all right?"

The vibration of Lucy's fingernails scraping the other side tickled my face.

"I know, little love," I whispered.

Mother let her out three days later, and none of us said a word about it.

* * *

"What do you think?" Lucy asked, twirling into our bedroom with her new frock. The stitching boasted little birds—blue swallows, soaring through cream linen.

"That's lovely," I told her.

"Swallows were her favorite creature." She gazed at the fabric, tracing a bird with her finger. Lucy would read Grandmother's journals every night before bed. I bought her other books, but she insisted the familiarity of Grandmother's words was the only thing to comfort her to sleep.

"Lucy," I said. "We've put aside more than enough to send you to London."

"What? Why on earth would we do that?" She crossed to the mirror to look at herself.

"This game must end eventually. We've enough money for both of us to do whatever we'd like. To get out of here."

"We are doing important work." She turned back to me with her fists on her hips. "We help people."

"Whom have we helped?"

"Whom have we helped?" There was an unfamiliar edge to her voice. "We provide closure." She brushed her hand over my sleeves, smoothing wrinkles with a rough yank.

"They speak with a spirit they do not know, who gives them vague postulations they can apply as they will. It is an opiate, that is all," I said, pushing her hands away. "I'm sending you to London with our earnings, and this act will end."

"Run a comb through this, will you?" She flicked a loose strand of my hair, then wrapped a finger around it and pulled it taut. "You cannot send me anywhere with money we do not have." Her eyes held mine defiantly.

I jerked my hair from her grip. "What are you talking about?"

She walked to her desk and opened a sketchpad, humming to herself.

"Lucy…" I muttered between gritted teeth as I hurried to the sewing kit hidden under my mattress. I flipped it open to see nothing but buttons and thread. "What have you done?"

She sat with her feet stretched before her, revealing new slippers beneath her new frock. My eyes traced from her feet to her desk that held wells of fresh ink, sheaths of crisp paper, colored pencils, decorative peacock feathers.

My mouth was hanging open, and I didn't know when it had dropped. I fell to a seat on the floor, the weight of my limbs suddenly too much for me to hold on my own. "How could you?"

She didn't look up, swiping long and delicate strokes with her pencil. "You cannot make me do anything."

And she was right. I became the famed medium, Lucy a permanent ghost.

One night, we received an urgent summons from an elderly woman by the name of Meryl Evans who had recently lost her husband. After an attempt on her own life, she reached out to us.

Lucy insisted we go to her at once.

The three of us gathered in her parlor—Meryl, myself, and Lucy hidden so well I hadn't seen where she'd gone. There were several lit lamps on the coffee table.

"Might we extinguish a few?" I asked.

"I have weak eyes," she croaked.

Lucy will just have to stay to the shadows then. I conjured Grandmother with little fanfare.

Lucy stayed behind my chair and talked with the woman about her husband. She made up messages from him that most men would likely want to give to their wives, and Meryl's hands never left her heart.

"Your husband is worried about you," Lucy said. She released my shoulders and walked toward her.

I snatched her skirt with two fingers, firmly enough for her to feel, but not so rough that Meryl would notice.

She took a hard step, ripping from my grasp. She sat with Meryl on the sofa and took her hand, not giving me a glance. Lucy didn't look like a spirit. She looked like a girl in pale makeup and an out-of-style gown.

The woman's old eyes were the only thing that saved us.

I dragged Lucy down the street to the cab by her elbow. "What was that?" I hissed. "If she had been younger than dust, we would have been found out!"

She said nothing, absently twisting the ring on her finger.

"Won't you answer me?"

Lucy stayed silent.

I wordlessly linked my fingers together and stooped for Lucy to drop her heel in. I hefted her up and watched her scuttle to the balcony.

We hadn't spoken since we left the old woman's house. It was fine by me. I had no clue what to say to her. I walked to the back door and waited.

I couldn't believe her behavior. It was so irresponsible. What if we were found out? What if it made a client angry and they came after us? What if they told Mother—God, what would she do about it?

I folded my arms against the cold and shuffled up the steps to press my ear to the door.

A voice carried on the wind—a yell.

I ran back around the house to the trellis.

Lucy's voice in our room, shouting. Mother's voice. I couldn't hear what they were saying, but I heard a crash.

"Lucy!" I jumped for the trellis but couldn't reach. "Open the door!" I ran to the front of the house and banged my fist against the wood. "Lucy, let me in!"

There was a scuffle upstairs, then a loud thunk on the foyer floor. I stepped back, a gasp choking me. I pressed my hand to my throat and whispered, "Lucy?"

The night grew colder on my shoulders. A moment later, the door opened.

Lucy stood before me, hair disheveled, fingers bloodied. And, for once, the blood was not her own.

"She has been losing her mind for some time." Lucy shook her head sadly. Her voice was so mature, so level.

The nurse nodded understandingly and offered a consoling rub down Lucy's arm.

Lucy told them Mother had jumped, and she gave a detailed history of Mother's erratic behavior. All of it true, a good bit of it certifiable by neighbors and workers, like the man who delivered our groceries and dealt with Mother's violent changes of mind, and the maid who often witnessed her ravings.

She rattled the list like it was rehearsed, and I just listened, no amount of blinking able to wipe the image of Lucy with bloodied hands standing in front of our mother, crumpled on the floor with her blue gown.

The nurse had questions about Mother's diet, medications, history—Lucy answered them all. Some information I didn't even know, and I wondered if she was making it up. She spoke with her hands and didn't scratch them once.

I watched Lucy from the door. Her content face, her graceful hands sweeping the sketchpad in front of her. She had decorated her room in pale blues and lace trimming that matched her gown— she looked like a cloud in a spring day.

"The act is over," I told her. "You will rejoin society before you are too old to marry, and that is the last word I'll have on it. We have no reason to carry on now."

"I was already married," Lucy said.

"What on earth are you talking about?"

"My husband, Edgar, was a wonderful man."

I bumped the side of my fist against the doorframe. "Grandpa Edgar locked her up—did you know that? He put her in an asylum, and she died in there. It isn't in her journals, because she never got to hold a pen again. Is that where you want to end up? You are *not* Grandmother."

Lucy's hand stilled, gripping her pencil.

"I refuse to continue the act. And you cannot do it without me. I will tell everyone it was a farce. If you refuse to go to school, that is fine, but you *will* resume your normal life."

"Honestly, child, you're raving," she said.

I crossed the room. "I beg you drop this." I knelt before her and took her hand. "You will give me gray hair before I am due for it," I said lightheartedly so she would know I was not angry.

Then I saw it. Grandmother's necklace around her throat. I stood. "Lucy—"

"I…am not…Lucy!" She screeched the last word, leaping to her feet and flinging her sketchpad across the floor. "My name is Alice Margrove! I was a general's daughter, and I died in childbirth for a beautiful boy named Reginald."

That was the moment I saw it, all at once. In her shimmering eyes and her clenched fists. Lucy wasn't there.

"Very well," I managed around the knot in my throat. I locked the door behind me and hurried down the stairs, away from the sound of Lucy slamming herself against the other side and wailing.

I called for the doctor and waited in the foyer, biting a hole in the inside of my cheek. I dropped my head against the wall to the beat of Lucy ramming the door. Then the sound shifted. Instead of the muted thump of her shoulders, hard and steady clunks rattled all the way to the wall at my back. Like she was beating a brick against the door. Or a skull.

"Lucy!" I ran back up the stairs two at a time and threw the door open.

Blood seeped from her forehead, bruises already forming around her eyes.

"What on earth are you doing!"

She shrieked and lunged at me, pinning me against the wall.

"Let me out," she muttered between clenched teeth. "Let me out. Let me out. Let me out, let me out, let-me-out-let-me-out-let-me-out."

I shoved as hard as I could, swinging her around into a two-arm grip and trapping her back against me. Her whole body vibrated.

"Lucy, please." Tears wet my face and fell into her hair.

She growled, feral and hateful. "My name isn't *Lucy,*" she hissed.

"Alice," I said.

Her shoulders shuddered, but she stilled.

"Alice, Alice, Alice," I cooed, still pinning her arms. "Alice, it's all okay. Help is coming."

A sigh rattled her body.

"The doctor is a nice man," I said. "We've seen him since we were girls, remember?"

Lucy's shuddering stopped, and I slowly released her. I led her to the balcony and opened the French doors wide, breathing in deep, exaggerating the motion. She mimicked me, taking big lungfuls of the spring breeze. I nodded, brushing a strand of hair from her face and tucking it behind her ear. Her wide brown eyes blinked at me, and I saw Lucy. My heart lifted, and I kept petting her hair. "It's all okay."

Lucy nodded, twisting her ring in slow loops.

"The doctor will know what is wrong with you."

That was not the right thing to say. Her eyes dropped to slits, and she shoved me.

My back slammed the balcony rail, cracking a loud snap that I wasn't sure was the plank or my spine. Lucy was upon me, all teeth and claws and dark eyes.

"Lucy!"

She shoved on my shoulders with every intention to fling me from the side. I threw my weight down. As I fell to a seat, she lunged again, and I planted a foot in her stomach to slow her, but she jumped too hard. She flew over my head, a white bird in a blue day.

I don't know how long I sat with my back to the splintered railing, staring into our bedroom, convincing myself that the sound had been a neighbor gardening, their spade burrowing in the dirt. Dogs tearing into a forgotten cut of meat. A sack of grain slapping into the bed of a wagon. A handful of twigs all snapping at once.

But eventually I stood. I walked the hall, past the room where my father died of fever, down the stairs where my mother fell to her end, and out the door to my sister.

There she was, splayed in the sunshine, taking an afternoon nap in a pool of blood.

I sat with her and held her hand, brushing curls from her face. Grandmother's necklace floated in crimson ink beside her. I unlatched the clasp and wiped the blue pendant clean.

The curtains of the balcony doorway fluttered in the air, alive until the wind faded, and they dropped.

I pushed the necklace to the bottom of my pocket.

BRUISING

The police station looms behind me, throwing shadows onto the concrete stairs. They morph and stretch the longer I look, wavering in the afternoon heat. The sidewalk seems miles away. I turn to the accessibility ramp and clutch the handrail the whole way down.

People pass on the street, smiling and talking at their phones and eating bagels, as if nothing has happened. They take no notice, like the officer who barely looked up while I gave my report, my hands in my lap and my mind shoved against the dirty carpet of a motel staircase.

I don't feel the pavement, but I watch it pass under my shoes. The streetlamps are taller than they usually are, I think—unsteady and shaking, ready to teeter and crush me. Every car horn and dog bark bites at my spine, every sound a screeched demand for me to leave because I shouldn't be here. I should have stayed home.

Sunset casts the town in hatred and shadows. A crow grips a powerline against a bruised red sky. His eye shines, watching me, waiting. The whole world looks evil, and I can't remember if it always has.

HOME

Eli grips the steering wheel of his Porsche 911. Staccato, erratic breaths rattle his lungs, burn his throat. He watches panic ripple in waves through tunneled vision, like the ocean sloshing when he was a kid with his eye pressed to a hole in the pier planks.

His phone dings, ten minutes over. He drags in a deep lungful, holds for five seconds, releases for seven.

After a few rounds of breathing, Eli's vision clears. He slides calm across his face and his phone into his jacket pocket, pulling the keys from the ignition with his other hand and stepping out of the car. He clicks it locked and crosses the street with swift, confident steps.

The house is brittled, slouching with age and neglect and spite.

He jams the key into the deadbolt and twists, but it sticks.

His hands stammer as he flips through his keys. They slip from his fingers and clunk to the porch.

He winces, eyes jumping to the curtained window, like she'd be watching him fumble. He swipes them and shoves in the right key, hurrying inside.

Light streams through thin slits of blinds, shooting beams of white into the particles Eli's entrance unsettles. Dust swirls like snowfall.

He leaves his shoes on the rack by the door and pads through the foyer, pressing the balls of his feet into faded floral. The carpet feels dirty under his black wool socks. He should have just kept his shoes on—she can't fuss him for it now. But he keeps walking.

The house breathes, calmer and steadier than Eli. He feels eyes watching through every turn of pattern in the wallpaper.

He buttons his suit jacket and forces himself not to walk faster.

Eli lets his eyes go out of focus until he enters the home office. Cobwebs drip from the ceiling fan blades, and the door sweeps a half-moon of clean hardwood in the gray carpet of dust. She hasn't been in this room in years.

A perfectly straight, categorized book collection lines the walls on floating shelves, and precisely placed office supplies dot the mahogany desk. He pulls a drawer open to reveal a flawless filing system.

There's a weight against his chest and between his shoulder blades while he flicks through papers. He isn't allowed in her office.

"She's dead," he says out loud. He pulls the house deed from a folder and sets it aside. She's dead, and she isn't coming back.

The smell of calamine lotion breezes past and disappears.

Eli's head snaps up.

He left the door open. He watches the hallway and imagines her walking past, shuffling in her slippers, hunched toward the floor.

He only visited the hospital once.

"We're keeping her comfortable. She's a sweet woman." The nurse smiled.

Eli stood over the bed and watched. She was small, wrinkled, sunk into the sheets like a fabric pin shoved too hard into a cushion.

A machine beeped slow.

"Do you want a moment alone?"

"No, I don't," he snapped, recognizing the bite in his voice but not as his own. "I'm going," he said, softer.

He wished he hadn't looked back. Her eyes were slit open, watching him leave.

Eli blinks. The hall is empty.

He slides the papers into a yellow folder and tucks it under his arm. There's nothing else for him here.

He crosses the street with long strides, his spine stretching, chin raising. His boot heels click the pavement. The sun is warm on his shoulders, and he won't look back. He slips behind the wheel, dropping the folder on his passenger seat and pulling from the curb.

But he does look back. Slit blinds watch him, and the house slouches a little further, sinking to the dirt.

MOTHER

A child was raised on stories of crows—dark creatures with black intentions. She'd know them by their raspy shriek, their crusted talons, their darting, evil eyes. She was warned that if she ever saw one, she should kill it. If she couldn't kill it, she should flee and say a thousand prayers, then a thousand more.

For as long as the child could remember, a friend visited her window. When she cried, it was there with a song, to rock her crib until she slept. As she grew, it brought gifts of gemstones, flowers, colorful silks, and all manner of lovely things.

Because its eyes were soft, its feathers sleek, and its song a calm whisper, the child was grown before she realized her friend was a crow. This was not a creature to hate and fear. "What have they done so wrong?"

Her question was an outrage, and she was locked away.

The crow appeared in her window before her first tear fell. "Would you like to leave now?" it asked in a mother's voice.

The girl stretched her wings wide, cracking off years of disuse, and they flew away.

STARLIT SHADOWS

Hard snow crunches under my shoes, loud with no echo. I step in the tracks I made on my way to the woodpile. Splinters tear at my thin sleeves, and the bark bites my palms.

The entryway to the kitchen ain't much warmer than outside. I wipe the snow from my shoes on the bristly mat and slip out my boots. Something about winter clears the air, and the staleness and mold smell a little sharper.

The house is quiet. I keep close to the wall and pad to the den. The room's empty and dark, flames from the fireplace licking shadows across the floor. I cross quick and stack the logs real careful.

The fire crackles. I stretch my hands in the warmth. The stiffness in my knuckles fades, and I imagine the snap of firewood is the sound of my bones defrosting, like when Mama throws hot water on the icy porch. My fingernails are jagged, dirt shoved under them that I can't scrub out. I close my fists.

"Did you chop them logs?" His deep, cracked voice shoots up my spine and shatters in my ears.

I stand up straight but don't turn from the fire.

"Did you chop them logs?" he says again. "Did you buy this house, with that fireplace in it?"

I swallow. My hands are still fists.

"Answer me, bitch."

"No, sir," I say.

"No, sir?" He's right behind me.

"No, sir, I ain't chopped them logs or bought this house with the fireplace in it."

"Then why you think you can use my property without my sayin' so?"

I'm not supposed to say nothing back. I hear myself and the fire breathing.

The burn of his palm on my head throws me down. I see his boots take two steps toward me. My pale hair hides my eyes, and I wish it could hide all of me.

He stands on my hand and slowly grinds it into the floor.

I wince and bite a whimper, keeping still as I can.

Mama glides past the doorway. We stare at each other—her eyes are still while mine leak pleas.

She walks off.

The air is heavy in my chest and I can't push it out. His foot presses harder until something snaps beneath it. Now I scream.

"S'what I thought." He kicks my hand at me.

I sit against the old barn with my hand in a pile of snow. My nose drips, and I wipe at it with the back of my good arm. I miss the crickets singing and moths pattering against windows. They'll be back, but for now it sure sounds lonely.

The stars peek in the dimming sun, and I'm glad for them, especially with the bugs gone. I think of summer. Of another year.

I lean and stretch my neck to see around the corner of the barn. Our cabin slumps in the yard. I imagine it collapsing on itself and everyone in it, but it stays standing.

"Anna," a voice whispers. Kathryn stoops beside me and looks at my hand in the snow. "What are you doing?"

I raise my arm to show her my bruised, swole fingers.

Kathryn sets her jaw. Her tan has paled away, but she'll be dark again when it's warm enough to swim. "Please let me tell my Pa. He'll get you out. And Johnny, I promise."

"No." I drop my head back to rest against the barn door. "When Johnny's big, he'll help us."

"He's a baby. You could be dead before then." Kathryn wraps her arms around her knees and watches me with the side of her face. "Who knows if he'll even get big? What if your father—"

"He ain't gonna hurt Johnny," I say sternly.

"You couldn't stop him if he wanted to."

I stand. "I can't stay today. I gotta cook dinner." He's already mad, and he hates having people around who ain't kin.

I peek around the barn. No one moves in the yard or windows. It's all clear. "Go in a straight line from the barn till you in the woods," I tell her.

She stares at me a minute but leaves without saying nothing. I watch until the skeleton trees swallow her up.

Johnny babbles, tugging on my legs. He pulls himself up to his feet and wobbles.

I smile at him. "Way to go, Johnny!"

He wobbles again, clutching my skirt with both hands. He gives me a drooly grin, brown eyes impossibly big for his face. I pat his curls and scoop him up. "The stove's hot," I say. "Stay over here a bit." I set him by his toys in the corner.

I pull Mama's big skillet onto the stove. It usually takes both hands and all my strength, but it's real tricky with a hurt hand. I manage, get it warming, and drop in a spoonful of lard. It sizzles and cracks, making me flinch.

"Annabelle!" His holler clanks like a shovel stamping gravel. The front screen door slaps shut.

I drop my spoon and rush to Johnny. I pull him into the pantry, kicking in a couple of his blocks. He ain't never fond of Johnny, but especially in this kinda mood. "Stay quiet now," I whisper, leaving the door cracked. Johnny doesn't like the dark.

"Yessir?" I call when I'm back to the stove, peeling open a can of meat with shaking hands. I swallow hard.

He lumbers in, dragging his right leg behind him—it was crushed years ago when he chopped down Mama's favorite tree 'cause she spilled a bottle of whiskey. He glares around the kitchen. I watch with the corner of my eye.

"Where's the little shit?" he grumbles.

"Crawling around someplace," I say, rattling my big stirring spoon around the pan a little louder than I need to, in case Johnny makes noise.

His foot drags the floor toward me, long and slow like a heavy winter wind, close enough to chill just with the sound of it.

I wrap my good palm around the skillet handle, my fingers not even reaching far enough to touch.

He's on my back. "What you cookin'?"

I grip the handle.

He leans over me and swipes a chunk of meat from the pan. I hear him eat it and suck the juice from his fingers. He stays pressed against me, and I watch the oil dance.

Mama walks in. She glances at us and drops her gaze.

I keep my head down at dinner. When I crawl into bed that night, I tuck Johnny in with me. We sleep in the window's moonlight, and I watch the stars.

That was six years ago. The winter Johnny opened the door himself, walked half a mile to an empty field, and fell asleep in the snow.

Moths patter against my window. The moon lights my face. I slide to the side of my mattress, into the dark.

I used to lay my long hair over the pillow, so I didn't roll on it, but Mama cropped it. I'd just started wearing my summer dress again—it fell above my knees 'cause my legs keep getting longer. I run a finger over the hair I have left. Mama said I had lice, and it was the only thing to be done.

A moth taps my window, harder and louder. It taps again. I sit up.

Kathryn's outside, cupping her hands around her eyes. She smiles at me and points to the back of the house.

My stomach slams my throat, and I wave for her to be quiet and go away, but the window's already empty.

The floor creaks under my bare foot when I step into the hall. I freeze and watch his bedroom door. When there ain't a shadow at the crack for a minute, I go on to the kitchen and silently slide the latch.

Kathryn waits with a smile. "You cut your hair!"

"Shh!" I inch the door shut. "You'll wake 'em."

She looks down. "Where are your shoes?"

I'm wearing thin flannel pajama bottoms and a worn-out tank top. I cross my arms over my chest. "What I need shoes for?"

"We're going camping." Kathryn pats the rucksack she's

holding. Her hair is braided back from her face.

"I can't leave," I whisper.

"They'll never know. I'll have you back before dawn, I swear."

I glance through the grimy window. The house is dark and still.

"Come on, Anna. It'll be fun, and you'll be back before they're awake."

A warm wind rustles the grass and curls around me, pulling me from the stoop, across the yard, through the woods, to the lake.

The moon shines off ripples, turning the water into a white sheet.

"Come on," Kathryn says. She picks her way along the rocky beach.

The shells poke the soles of my feet. "The rocks are sharp," I tell her.

Kathryn doubles back and crouches down in front of me. I jump on her back and she walks. Kathryn's short and stocky, and she carries me easy. My limbs have stretched the past year, but I keep getting skinnier.

Rocks crunch under her shoes and echo over the water. The crickets sing. "Here we go," she says.

I hop onto a smooth, flat rock. Kathryn must have been here earlier, 'cause there's a little campfire glowing.

She climbs up too, and we scoot close to the flames. "Look what I brought," she says. She pulls a plastic bag of puffy white marshmallows from her rucksack.

I've never had one, but I've seen them advertised on his television when I watch from the hall.

Kathryn tears the bag open with her teeth and threads three marshmallows onto a thin switch. She holds them over the fire.

"I've missed you," I say, speaking low, like we're still in earshot of the cabin. "How was your term?"

"It went well," Kathryn says. "Honor roll and all. But I'm amped to be home."

Four months is such a long time. I imagine what it's like—miles away, no rules. Friends. Kathryn's wearing thick denim shorts—she must have bought them either this summer or the one before. No bare threads, no patches.

"Here." She pulls a browned marshmallow from the tip of her switch and passes it to me. "It's hot," she says. "Be careful."

It feels harder than it looks. I squeeze and it crunches. I push the whole thing into my mouth and the sweet burning liquid has already spread across my tongue when Kathryn's eyes widen and she says, "No, don't just—"

My mouth drops open and the marshmallow splats onto the rock next to me. I look at her in horror.

Kathryn barks a laugh, and I laugh with her. We laugh until my sides ache and eyes water, then we're lying on our backs, watching the sky. The moon has set and the stars pierce.

"How long will you stay here?" Kathryn's voice is soft.

"I have to be back before the sun's up," I tell her.

"No." She sits up and looks at me. "How long will you stay *here*."

"This is my home."

"You're nearly grown. You'd be graduating school in a year, if they'd let you go. My folks said you haven't even been to church since last summer."

Mama said my church dress wasn't good no more, and we can't afford a new one. She didn't like the way it fell on me. It was inappropriate. "I've been busy keeping up the house is all. Roof keeps leaking."

"Johnny's gone," she whispers. "Nothing's keeping you."

I don't say nothing.

Kathryn takes my hand. "I'm worried. 'Specially with me being gone at school. You don't have anyone else."

"I've got the stars," I say.

Kathryn lays back again and sighs.

"They're here every night. I'm never really alone."

"There's more life out there," Kathryn says. "More than surviving the day to see the stars."

We lay in silence and watch each other—me and Kathryn and the sky. I met Kathryn on a night a lot like this one, but a lot different too.

Mama had screamed in the yard. I held a towel and watched.

She squatted with her knees as high as her face and dug her nails into the big cherry tree. She yelled loud, but that's not the sound I'd remember best. It was the squelching slurp of Johnny sliding out and rolling onto the ground.

Then he got to screaming too.

Mama scooped him up and fell back, crying. He nursed and we cleaned him up in the kitchen sink, and I remember Mama's face falling further and further the more she wiped off him.

"Annabelle," she told me serious, knelt down to look me in the eye. "Your Papa will be back tomorrow." She swallowed, clutching Johnny to her chest. "I'ma need you to do something real important, okay?"

I nodded.

"You take him out somewhere, far enough we can't hear him crying. He's gonna cry. You keep him out there as long as you can, okay? You hear me? At least two days. We'll pack you some food… and…" Mama's eyes went glassy. She pushed Johnny into my arms and moved stiffly around the kitchen, filling a basket.

That night, I was hurrying across the yard with the basket burning my arms. Halfway to the river, I put it on the ground and pulled it along behind me. It was full of food and bottled milk and a big blanket with Johnny on top, and it was heavy.

The river was my favorite hideaway. He was scared of water, so he'd never find me there.

Mama was right—Johnny did cry that night. I had to sit on the ground with him in my lap to hold him with my tiny arms. He wouldn't take to the bottle, but I'd dipped the corner of the blanket in milk, and he sucked on that. His cries quieted, and his eyelashes fluttered.

"It's okay," I whispered. "I'm not gonna let nobody hurt you."

Johnny sighed and fell asleep in my arms.

A splash woke me right before dawn, and I jerked up to a seat. Johnny was laying still in the basket. I checked he was breathing and touched his cheek with one finger.

The splash had come from a girl, tossing rocks across the river a bit down the bank.

"Hey!" I said.

She looked up and waved, smiling big.

Kathryn sat with us and we watched the stars fade. She's the one told me Johnny was different, that his dark skin meant he wasn't my kin.

"What does that mean?"

"Means your Mama been busy." Kathryn and I sat side by side, and she had her chin propped on her shoulder, watching me. "Any men coming around your house?"

"No," I said quickly. "We don't have no visitors. He don't like 'em."

"No visitors at all?" Her eyebrows pinched together. "Do you go to school?"

I shook my head.

"So you never see no one but your parents?"

"Well, we got Johnny now." I pulled his basket closer and watched his eyelids flutter in sleep.

"And me," Kathryn said firmly. "We're gonna be friends forever." She took my hand and smiled.

When I went home, Mama was busted up and bruised, but he was quiet and didn't look at me or Johnny. Mama told me keep

Johnny out his sight as much as I could, and she never looked at Johnny neither.

But Kathryn was wrong. Johnny *was* kin, and I held him close every day until that winter when he fell asleep in the snow.

Kathryn waves from the treeline and disappears as I slip into the kitchen. I slide the lock back and freeze—if anyone had woken in the night and seen the door unlatched, they would have checked my bed and seen I was gone. I exhale and tiptoe for my room, stepping over loose floorboards.

"Annabelle," he says from a shadowed corner.

The sides of my vision darken, and I can't move.

"You think I'm stupid?"

I don't look, but I know Mama is sitting next to him with her hands around a mug of coffee, looking through me. Her coffee is cold. It always is, but she won't drink it anyway. She never does.

"I'm talkin' to you." He's behind me and his voice is around my throat like a fist, choking the air that fights to get to my lungs. If the floor could swallow me up, I think it would, outta mercy.

I turn with slow steps.

His chest takes up my whole vision. "You think you can sneak out at night and get fucked in the woods by some negro boys and I won't know?"

His hand crashes the side of my skull, but I stay standing.

"You think you smarter than us? You come back with a

bastard in your belly and think I'll let it grow to eat our food and starve us?"

He bends me forward by my shoulders, slams a knee into my belly, and shoves me away.

I stumble until I bump into the stove. It's cold and hard, and I brace myself against it. The words burn my throat before I even say them. "He wouldn't eat your food, 'cause you'd just leave him out to freeze. And you'd let him, wouldn't you, Mama?"

A sliver of dawn slips into the kitchen from the only window still covered in glass, touching my parents. The soft, orange light strokes Mama's crumpled face, laces its fingers through her knotty hair, lights up her eyes—the same blue as mine, but dull and grayed and defeated. They used to shine. She'd watched from the window when I buried Johnny in the yard. I remember the weight of Johnny's body in my arms. You wouldn't think a baby could be so heavy.

He slumps to one side, favoring his right leg as he stalks toward me and his shadow grows. But he ain't as tall as he used to be.

I feel Mama's skillet on the stove behind me. My fingers are long enough to wrap the handle now.

His hand raises, but mine's quicker. The soft thump of the skillet hitting his skull ain't the sound I imagined.

He crumples.

And I run.

I jump from the kitchen door, off the porch. I tear across the yard, into the thicket, and the only sounds are my feet ripping the earth and my lungs pulling air. Trees whiz past, a branch slapping my arm. It bleeds, but I don't feel it, and I don't slow down.

Golden rays warm my face and set the woods glowing. The sun is full risen.

WHITE RABBIT

Maya's throat burns, but she won't cry. She swallows and pushes dirt over the little rabbit, dark soil covering white fur until it disappears.

Maya adopts all sorts of animals. People will abandon anything. Cats, dogs, rabbits, fish, rats. Their lives pass in blinks. Her yard is full of tiny, unmarked graves.

She's raised parrots before. They live a little longer than the rest, which just makes it harder. Her first was a hatchling. Eve had left it on her doorstep after Roscoe, the thirty-ninth dog, passed. The hatchling was stolen from its nest too soon. With pricks of pin feathers and gray-lidded eyes, it died in her hands.

She straightens and shakes dark hair out of her face before stepping on the loose grave. The toe of her boot sinks into dirt.

Maya slides her fork along the ceramic plate, relishing the muted screech above the voice of the woman across from her.

"Oh, God." Sabrina presses a finger to her temple and chuckles. "That's like nails on a chalkboard."

Maya drops her fork and folds her hands. "I'm sorry. You were saying?"

Sabrina takes off on her story again, about backpacking across Europe (Germany) four summers ago (it was life-changing). Maya can't imagine Sabrina is much different than she had been before those two weeks in Germany, but she tries to listen to the story anyway.

Sabrina runs fingers over her blonde undercut and doesn't hold Maya's gaze while she talks. Her eyes flutter the restaurant, easily distracted by any movement or sound, like a toddler. She's a small woman, and if she slumped Maya would only be able to see her head over the table.

Maya exhales. "I'm sorry," she says, pushing her chair out. "I'm really not feeling well." She leaves Sabrina with a hundred-dollar bill on the table and an, "It was great meeting you."

She taps at her phone as she trots down the restaurant steps, flipping through Matchr profiles. An alert blinks. An older man— Gabriel, with a full beard, a big dog, and what looks like his own backyard—reached out with, *Impressive taste in music. I can show you some new stuff in the same vein sometime.*

How's tomorrow? Maya types back before slipping her phone into her pocket.

The streets are quiet. She stops under a tree and sighs, toeing a puddle of rainwater to watch the moonlight ripple. "I can smell you."

Eve's clean red sneakers drop from above and land next to the puddle. Maya glances up. Eve's a few inches shorter than Maya, but her natural glower makes it feel like she towers above. Her pale hair is swept into what Maya calls her hunting ponytail.

"Why are you doing this?" Eve asks in a voice too deep for her size.

"Doing what?"

Eve hisses between her teeth. "You're wasting your time."

Maya shoulder-checks her and continues down the street. "Good thing I've some to spare."

Gabriel is a few years older than he looked in his pictures, which is fine. Preferable, honestly.

"Maya?" He smiles when he opens the door. "Come in! You look great."

Maya tucks a braid behind her ear, stepping into his living room. She's wearing jeans and her bright yellow sweater. She does look great in yellow. "You have a nice house." It looks cleaner than it smells. A sleeve pokes from under the couch cushion. "Where's your dog?"

"Hm? Oh, that was my buddy's dog."

"Ah. Do you have any pets?"

"Fuck no." He plops onto the couch and pats the cushion beside him.

She sits. "Don't like animals?"

"No time for that kind of stuff." He scratches his beard.

She glances around for a kitchen. He had said he'd cook. "What's for dinner?"

"Oh, are you hungry?" He leans forward to grab his phone from the coffee table. "We could order something up."

"Or we could go out," she says.

"Aren't you more comfortable inside?" He slides toward her. "We can order some pizza afterward."

"After what?"

He chuckles. "We met on Matchr."

"I just wanted to have dinner tonight," she says. Not that she hasn't had sex on a first date before, but she definitely isn't feeling it right now. She stands. "Sorry if that was unclear. I'll just head out."

"No, no," he says, pulling her back by the wrist. "Hey, we're all good. Let's order a pizza, and I can put on a movie."

This will go one of two ways. Either works. She sits.

Gabriel flicks through the movie selection. "What're you into?"

"I like documentaries, action, historical, romance—"

He snorts. "Okay, let's see." He clicks a title Maya doesn't recognize, which is odd. She's seen every movie on both of her streaming services. He must have bought this one.

The movie plays for a few minutes, but Maya's eyes wander his living room, picking up smudges and piles of dust and long-forgotten paperwork shoved into random spots. Maya keeps her house pristine, her lawn neatly mowed. She doesn't do well in untidy spaces. It's always been a problem for her, even before.

But Gabriel's hand on her knee snaps her out of it. "What do you think?"

She looks back to the TV, where two women are half-naked, crawling all over each other. He put on porn. Charming.

He slips his hand up and squeezes her thigh. "Are you ticklish?"

"No."

He chuckles. "I think you're lying."

"Please stop."

"Aw, come on." He laughs and brings both hands to her waist. "I know you're ticklish."

She takes a firm grip on his wrists.

His eyes darken and he flips his hands around to grab her the same way, dragging her arms up to pin them against the back of the sofa. "You like to be rough?"

She tugs, but he squeezes them tighter.

"I'm going to ask you one more time," she says. "I would like to leave. Please let me go."

He pushes her hands into the cushions and drops his face into the crook of her neck. "Why are you talking like that—you a robot?"

She watches the ceiling. "No." She waits, just a few more seconds, before slipping her hands from his grip and shoving him onto the coffee table.

"What the fuck—"

She drops her fangs so he can see them. Fear flavors people, she's always thought. Might just be in her head. She straddles his thighs and yanks him up by the collar of his shirt. "You like to be rough?"

Maya leaves Gabriel in his living room. She used to keep up with the mess, but there's really no point. Her DNA isn't on any record. Her name isn't even in the system. She died a hundred years ago.

Under a porch light, a child with tight curls and chunky cheeks laughs and stumbles in front of her, chasing a leaf in the wind. He totters, nearly falling, but Maya's hand is there to steady him. He doesn't acknowledge her and breaks back into an awkward run.

The mother nods at her from the porch steps, and Maya stops to watch the little boy a moment longer.

She's considered adoption, filling the hole in her heart with a child to watch them grow and die. She could raise and turn them when they were old enough to decide. But no, she would have conditioned them for it—that is not a choice either.

He finally catches the leaf and brings it to his mother, beaming with pride. The mother smiles, tucking it into her purse.

Maya leaves them, walking home with the company of her footsteps. When she turns onto her street, she sighs. "Stop following me."

Eve is in front of her, walking backward. "I heard everything in that apartment." She stops, forcing Maya to stop too. She reaches a hand to Maya's face, swiping at the side of her mouth. Her thumb comes away bloody.

Maya hurriedly wipes her sleeve across her face, wondering if the mother saw it.

Eve examines the blood and wrinkles her nose. She rubs it on the leg of her jeans. "I'll hunt for us. You don't have to debase yourself for bitter meals."

"*You* can seduce young girls to their deaths. That will never be me." She shoves her away.

"You let them demean you—"

"I let them earn it, and I rest easy."

Eve's voice is uncharacteristically soft. "When will I be enough?"

Maya leaves the answer hanging in the dark behind her.

"I exist for you," Eve calls. "I will wait however long it may take for our lives to begin together." She is right behind her.

Maya spins. "You robbed me. Of everything! I watched my parents die. I watched my baby brother forget his own name. I followed his children from their christenings to their graves."

"You've never been alone. And you never will be." She brushes a hand over Maya's hair. "I didn't just pick you at random, you know. I watched, for years. I didn't consider turning you until it began." She sets a finger against Maya's temple, where two strands of gray nestle in black. "You never fit in with them, even when you were one of them. I couldn't watch you slip to dust." She takes Maya's hand, pressing it to her own cheek. "I will wait. However long."

Maya walks away, pulling herself from Eve's grip. "You will wait an eternity."

The next gift on Maya's doorstep isn't a hatchling parrot. Eve stands, blood wiped down the side of her face and neck, a limp woman hooked in one arm. She throws her forward, and Maya lunges to catch her.

"What did you do?" Maya hisses.

"This is Abigail," Eve says, her toes to the edge of the threshold. "She double-majored at Vassar, minored in anthropology, studied abroad every summer on trips she funded with three part-time jobs. She volunteers her weekends at more charities than I could keep track of. She likes documentaries and the cooking channel, her favorite color is yellow, and she'll die if you don't change her."

Abigail's face is pale, and her half-closed eyes stare at nothing. Maya drops her fangs, whipping to face Eve. "You can't use people like playthings! This is a person."

"She won't be a person for long, either way." Eve folds her arms. "Make a choice."

Maya presses her hands to the wound on Abigail's neck, but she's bleeding from her hip too. And her leg. Her pulse is so weak it's barely there at all.

"You're the devil," Maya whispers. "You have no soul, and nothing can save you."

Eve squats on the porch to look her in the eye. "But you can save her."

Maya runs a finger from Abigail's cheek to the soft of her throat. She can save her.

Maya slams the back of her shovel against the biggest grave she's ever dug and drops it, wiping dirt from her palms.

The stars shine on her invisible graveyard.

She makes a mug of lavender tea and watches the long mound of dirt from her window. Abigail rests in an unmarked grave with the bones of rats and snakes and Roscoe the dog for company.

She chugs her tea and drops the mug in the sink. It shatters. Maya presses her hands against the countertop and watches the shards glitter moonlight.

Then that too-familiar bitterness stings her nose, and she leaves the broken mug to follow it to her front door. She opens it wide.

"Eve," Maya says to the night.

She is before her in a blink.

She watches Eve's round eyes and still hands and the expectant quirk of her mouth. Maya's jaw clenches as she swallows hard and steps aside. "Come in."

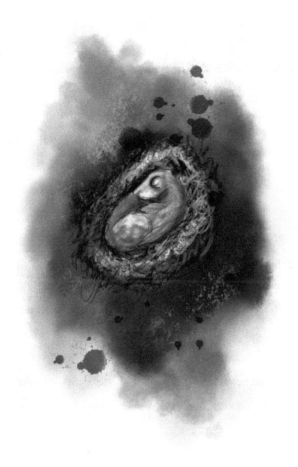

PASSING GHOSTS

I had felt Marcus' footsteps pounding down the stairs and heard him calling my name, but I knew he'd never touch me again. I saw how fast the blood was spreading. My face was wet with it, pressed into the ugly laminate tile. I faded before he reached me.

I sit on the countertop now, watching that yellowed, dingy flooring. It's crumbled, tossed in a pile on a tarp. I'm happy to see it go after thirty years.

After Marcus left, the house was empty. The weeks and months floated by like nothing—the emptiness was better than watching him drink himself unconscious.

Every spring, a family of squirrels would nest in the attic, and I watched the babies grow. When someone put the house on market, they sealed the hole and the squirrels haven't been back.

Now I share the house with a family of three. I rub my hand on my belly—the family we almost had, but I'm glad we didn't. I don't think about what a child would have done here without me, with him. I'm glad she stayed safe inside. Sometimes I think I can still feel her, but I doubt that's how it works. She's in heaven, I tell myself. I'm stuck in my own purgatory.

The little boy is fourteen. He comes down the stairs, hops right onto the spot I died. I like the dark wood floors.

He pads to the fridge and I study his face in the soft glow. Red brows bush out over pale gray eyes and freckle-scattered skin. His jaw is already defined and cut at sharp angles, but his cheeks are still round with childhood. Andrew, they call him. I call him Andy.

He pulls out a bag of shredded cheese and pours it directly into his mouth. A few pieces scatter on the floor.

I chuckle, and he chokes. His head whips around.

"Mom?" He glances back at the stairs. The light in the hall shines down. He pushes the cheese back into the drawer without zipping it and hurries to his bedroom, taking two steps at a time.

I pace the hall at night, watching over them. I know I can't do anything if they need help, but I still like to see they're safe. Glynn and Samantha are trying for another child. She has baby fever. I excuse myself from their room. I watched a few times, just for something to do, but that made me feel pretty grody, so I haven't in a while.

I sit with Andy. He's playing a video game, and I'm amazed at how real it looks. His character is a soldier, mowing down enemy troops. The splatters and screams make me wince, but Andy doesn't blink.

They have a cat, Elvira. She sneaks outside at night to visit with another cat in the yard. I watched them a few times too, through the window—that got old. I hope she has kittens, but I think she's spayed. I've tried to look for a scar on her belly, but she's fluffy and doesn't roll over often. I miss the squirrels.

I float back to the master bedroom. Glynn and Samantha aren't touching anymore, settled onto their opposite sides of the bed.

Samantha talks on the phone a lot in the afternoons, to her mom, complaining about Glynn being distant, an incompetent father, not loving her as much as he should.

I've seen him tuck the sheet around her shoulders at night. He leaves for work before the sun is up and comes back in time for a late dinner, if Samantha has saved him any. He washes dishes but doesn't mention it when she yells at him for not helping out enough.

I check on Andy, and he's in bed now. It's nearly two o'clock. I don't like when he stays up this late. But he isn't sleeping. I hear him whimper.

I sit with him and sing the song Mama would sing to me when it thundered and I'd crawl into bed with her.

Andy bolts upright, breathing heavy. "Hello?" he whispers.

"Hey, Andy." I'm whispering too. I raise my voice a little. "I won't hurt you. I'm a friend."

He turns his head my way, but I can tell he's looking through me.

"Can you hear me?"

He stares at the wall, blinking tears. A heavy moment passes. But slowly, he nods. If I could breathe, I would stop now. He can hear me. He knows I'm here. I press my fists hard in my lap and sit up straight, taming my excitement.

"Can you see me?" I ask.

His eyes trace the wall and window.

I wave my hand in front of his face. "I won't hurt you," I say. "You don't have to be afraid."

He swallows and nods once.

"I've been here with you the whole time." I don't know why I told him that. He's wigged enough as it is.

He finally speaks. "What's your name?"

"Caroline."

"Are you an angel?"

Am I an angel? "I don't think so."

"Are you...good?"

Disappointing daughter, high school dropout, Marcus' girlfriend, an accidental mother. Almost mother. "I try to be."

"Were you a person?"

"Yes."

He pauses. "What happened to you?"

I left a towel on the bathroom floor and my boyfriend threw me down the stairs. "I fell down the stairs."

I can see the whites of his eyes in the dark. "Our stairs?"

"Yeah."

"I'm so sorry," he says.

"That's okay," I say, lamely. I clear my throat—it doesn't do anything, but some habits didn't stay with my body. I wonder where my body is.

"How old are you?" he asks. "Or, how old were you when you died?"

"Nineteen." I rest my palm on my belly.

Andy lays back on his pillow. "Do you need to do anything?" He props a hand behind his head and watches the ceiling.

"What do you mean?"

"Don't ghosts get trapped in houses when they need revenge or something?"

I shrug a shoulder. He can't see me. "I don't know," I say. I lay next to him and watch the ceiling too. "Haven't really thought about it."

I was never angry at Marcus. He didn't do anything out of the ordinary—it just happened to kill me that time. I think of the baby I never got to see in my own silhouette. She's better off anywhere else than with me.

"I don't feel rushed," I say. "I just feel...like this is where I am. Like there's nothing to worry about."

"Can I get you anything?" he asks. "Some books or a movie? Do you need me to give a message to your parents?"

I haven't seen Mama since I was fifteen. Never met my father. "No," I say. "No messages."

"Well, let me know if you need anything?" He rolls to his side, facing me but probably not realizing. "I know how it feels to be trapped." He falls asleep, content and quiet, like he wasn't just talking to a dead girl.

All I do when Andy's gone is wait for him to come home. When he is home, I try not to bother him. We both pretend I have anything else to do. My busy, dead girl schedule.

I wait outside his bedroom in the morning, and I sit with him at breakfast to make snarky comments to Samantha that only he can hear. It makes him smile. I wish him luck at school when he leaves, then I stay scarce when he gets home.

We have a secret code when he's ready to talk—he fake sneezes. I say "bless you" outside his door before I enter. It's dumb, but it makes me smile. He smiles too.

Sometimes I can help with his homework—I still understand math and geography and a few others, but science is something he teaches me. I read the textbook over his shoulder, way more invested in it than he is.

"What do you do when I'm gone?" he asks one day.

"I watch Elvira," I say. "She mostly naps and eats. Sometimes I follow your mom around."

"Are you bored?"

"Not really. I know you'll be home in a few hours." I shrug. "I used to watch nests of squirrels up in the attic. Looking at the same thing for weeks is something I'm pretty good at."

"You watched squirrels grow?"

"Mm-hm."

Andy crosses his bedroom and shakes the mouse of his desktop computer. It springs to life and he types something that I don't read because I'm watching his fingers. They move so quickly over the keys that it doesn't look like he could possibly be hitting them in any order.

"Look," he says. He pulls up a video of a bird nest.

"What is this?"

"A live feed of golden eagle eggs. They set up these webcams and stream twenty-four hours a day. There are tons of them, look." He clicks to another page. "Bear cubs in the Saint Ann Sanctuary, hummingbird feeders in Costa Rica. Here's an underwater one. Do you like sea lions?"

I hunch in front of the screen, mesmerized. There are hundreds of video feeds of animals and natural wonders from all over the world. There's a geyser, spewing white foam into the air, a glowing orange lava flow ebbing through a stone valley.

"Is that a waterfall?"

He clicks the waterfall video and it covers the whole screen. "This is a part of Niagara Falls," he says. "I think it's recording from a boat."

I've always wanted to see Niagara Falls. "This is amazing," I breathe.

Andy keeps his face toward the screen, but he smiles wide. We click through footage for the rest of the afternoon.

He always remembers to put one on before he leaves.

I'm waiting in the foyer when Andy gets home from swim practice.

I slip next to him and match his pace. "She's mad."

He rolls his eyes and mutters, "What'd I do now?"

Samantha perches on a stool at the island counter, flipping through a glossy catalogue with one finger, her eyes already on Andy.

"Did you have a good practice, Andrew?" Her voice is flat and expectant.

"Yes, ma'am." Andy slips his shoes into the holder by the hall closet and walks into the kitchen.

She flips another page she didn't look at. "Anything you'd like to tell me?"

"No, ma'am," Andy says.

I pull myself onto the counter, tucking my knees under my chin and watching her catalogue. Swimsuits aren't something I've thought about in a long time, but they sure look different now. I look at my clothes and body. Cuffed blue jeans, scuffed Converse, a plain yellow tee. If I'd known this was the outfit I'd be stuck in for the rest of eternity, I would have worn something cooler.

Samantha slaps the magazine shut, and I flinch.

"Mrs. Treul called." She raises her eyebrows.

Andy shrugs. "What'd she want?"

"She *wanted* to tell me what her son has been up to."

Andy and I wait. After a moment, I say, "Does she want us to guess?"

He smiles.

"What's funny?" Samantha shoves her stool out and stands.

"Nothing, Mom," he says quickly. "What did Toby do?"

"He and some boys from the team have been getting his cousin to buy them alcohol. And I can see from your face that you're one of them."

Andy shakes his head. "I don't know anything about it."

"You're lying!" she screeches.

I tuck my ear to my shoulder, but Andy stands straight.

"I want your Xbox on this table," she presses her pointer finger into the countertop until it turns white, "and your father will have a piece of you when he gets home."

"Mom, I didn't—"

"I WILL NOT REPEAT MYSELF."

"Don't make promises you can't keep," I mutter, wishing she could hear me. I slip to the floor. "Come on, Andy."

We go to his room. He wordlessly wraps the cords around his game and brings it to the kitchen, where Samantha and her finger still wait.

She steps her toes to his. "I don't want to see your face again tonight." She points to his room, and we file back into it.

Andy lies on his bed and drapes his arm over his forehead. I sit beside him.

"Have you been drinking?" I ask.

"No."

"It's okay," I say, "if you were. I did before I died, and I was underaged." And I guess I always will be. "If I hadn't done it then, I never would have." I try to say it like a joke, but it doesn't really come out as one.

"I haven't," he says.

I believe him. He's a good kid, always following the rules. His eyes are sad.

"I'll be right back," I tell him.

The lights are dim in the living room. Samantha is kicked back in an armchair, resting her hand over her eyes. Elvira is perched in her lap.

I float to the cat. I've never been able to touch anyone, but animals usually know I'm here.

Elvira opens her eyes in a slow blink and looks right at me. I hiss, contorting my face into the most hideous thing I can muster, and it works. She screeches, digging claws into Samantha's white capri pants before launching off the chair and bolting from the room.

I'll have to make amends with Elvira later, but hearing Samantha scream and seeing spots of blood speck her snow-white pants is worth it.

I rush back because I know Andy will come to check on her. "She doesn't want to see your face for the rest of the day," I remind him as I breeze back into his room.

Glynn doesn't scold Andy for anything that night, despite Samantha's insistence. That's typically how it happens. I keep watch while Andy sneaks into the kitchen to grab food and retreat to his room with it.

Samantha stews on the back porch, sneaking cigarettes everyone knows she smokes. I stand at the door and watch her, trying to find answers on her face. How could someone have a child they don't treasure? Maybe it's something only mothers can know.

Andy leaves for college, and I am so proud.

I watch his parents' marriage crumble without him. I miss Glynn when he leaves.

Now it's me and Samantha. And Elvira, of course. I talk to Elvira a lot. I wish she could talk back, but she's a good listener, and that works for me.

Waiting for Andy to visit during breaks is the first I've felt of time's weight. The hours tick by like months. I wish I could sleep.

Andy is finally home. I'm curled on the foot of his bed like a cat, listening to him talk. He is so different already. Freedom has grown him. I like the stubble on his face and the way he talks with his hands, emphasizing his words, miming his stories. He is older than me now.

He has friends and a part-time job at the campus coffee shop.

He's learning to play piano. His eyes dance until Samantha walks in.

Her voice slurs and her eyes are bloodshot. "You come all the way home to see *me* and spend the whole time on the phone?"

His hands clench in his lap. "Sorry, Mom," he says. "I'll be out in a minute."

She huffs and leaves the door open. Andy's eyes search in my direction. He extends an open palm.

I ghost my hand on his, pretending it feels warm.

He walks to his door, a little boy again.

"Go on," I say. "I'll be here when you come back."

After Andy graduates, he visits often.

Samantha drinks more when she knows he's coming, and she slams drawers and cabinets a little harder, like she's warming up.

My heart breaks the day I tell him he doesn't have to do it anymore. He doesn't listen at first, but his visits slow until they trickle to an end.

He taped pictures of himself to the inside of his closet— from when he was a curly-haired, cow-eyed baby to his cap and gown portraits. The most recent is from his trip abroad, holding a pint of beer and a wide grin. I sit on the carpet and watch the photos on lonely days. Most days.

Sometimes he calls Samantha's cellphone when he knows she's sleeping and leaves voicemails. I stand close when she listens to them.

"I love you," he says. "Thank you for everything."

Samantha returns his calls, but he never answers.

The house is empty again. Abandoned furniture peppers every room, draped in gray and white sheets, like lonely ghosts. That thought only makes me laugh once.

There aren't squirrels to watch. Roaches skitter at night, and sometimes the rain will bring in a line of ants. The ants don't stay for long.

Andy cracks the front door and peers in. He is handsome and tall and the hair over his ears is just turning from red to gray.

"Andy…" My voice is a whisper, like I have a throat that could become dry and scratchy from years of disuse. I rest a hand on his shoulder. It slips through when he steps into the house.

"Caroline?" he calls quietly.

"I'm here." I step in front of him.

His eyes scan the kitchen.

I trail behind to the living room, to his bedroom, to Samantha's. We weave together through sheeted tombs of armchairs and coffee tables, his shoes stirring clouds of dust—I step in his footprints. He stares into the backyard, and I stare with him.

I sit in his bedroom window and watch his car pull from the curb.

"I'm still here," I say.

It's a bit louder now, the silence.

But he comes back, and my heart is light. He brings his wife, Deja—she is beautiful—and a baby. A beautiful, perfect baby. I lean over him, memorizing his tiny features. His eyes follow me.

I feel my belly. It's just my own flesh. But, no, it's not even that.

They call the baby Micah, and so do I. His eyes and hair are black like Deja's, but he has Andy's freckles.

Andy sleeps with his arm across Deja's ribs, and she brings him coffee in bed every morning. He still wakes in the middle of the night sometimes, and I follow to the kitchen to watch him eat leftovers from the container with his fingers, the fridge light smoothing his features and softening the years.

Micah is fussy about staying in his own bed, so I sing to him.

He is almost two when he says my name. "Cah-wo-yine."

We're playing on the living room floor, and I'm rawring the voice of the dinosaur he holds.

I sit up. "Did you say Caroline?" My face cannot hold my grin.

Andy is bent over the stove, cooking dinner, but he heard it. He abandons the pot to simmer and crosses to us with long, slow steps. He squats beside Micah. "Hey, buddy. What'd you say?"

Micah claps his hands. "Cah-wo-yine!"

Andy swallows, and he smiles. His gaze searches the room, face aged with laugh lines, with life-lived lines. The freckles are long tanned away, but gray eyes nearly see me.

I stare back, and I smile with him.

He knows I'm here. That is more than enough.

THANKS

It might not take a village, but sometimes it takes a couple pals.

Thank you to my writing partners, Micah and Gloria, for the laughs, late-night writing sessions, and for making a solitary job a little less lonely.

To my editor, Krys, for working with me through nine versions of the same story with an unshakably great attitude and fresh jokes for every revision.

To my patrons and subscribers for their support, in the very many forms it comes in.

And thank you to my readers (even the ones who leave me stinky reviews). Couldn't be here without y'all.

AUTHOR

Hannah Lee Kidder is a contemporary and fantasy author, writing coach, and YouTuber. She published her first short story collection, *Little Birds*, in 2018.

Hannah is currently minding her own business somewhere in the Colorado mountains with her roommate, Saya, who is a dog.

Also by Hannah Lee Kidder

Little Birds

A collection
of
short stories

by
Hannah Lee Kidder
Illustrations by Rosalyn Stilling